First published in the United States 1989 by E. P. Dutton,
a division of Penguin Books USA Inc.
Originally published 1988 by bohem press,
Zurich, Switzerland

Designer: Martha Rago
First American Edition
Printed in Hong Kong by South China Printing Co.
ISBN: 0-525-44546-3   10 9 8 7 6 5 4 3 2 1

TALES OF A LONG AFTERNOON

five fables and one other retold by Max Bolliger

paintings by Jindra Čapek

❖

translated by Joel Agee

E. P. DUTTON   NEW YORK

One beautiful afternoon,
eight animals met in a meadow
in the middle of the woods:
a fox and a raven,
a turtle and a hare,
a peacock and a crow,
a wolf and a dog.

The sun was shining,
and the animals decided
to have a party.
There was plenty to eat
and plenty to drink.
The peacock spread his tail.
The raven and the crow
tried to sing.

The fox, the turtle,
the hare, the wolf,
and the dog
danced to the music,
each in his own way.

Though no two animals
were alike,
they all had
a wonderful time together.

When evening came
and the sun began to set,
one of them proposed
that each one tell a tale.

The first tale
was told by the fox.
It went like this:

THE FOX AND THE RAVEN

There once was a raven who had stolen a piece of cheese.

He settled on a pine branch, pleased to have found such a tasty treat.

But just as he was about to swallow it, a fox came walking along. He had smelled the cheese from afar.

"Good evening, Mister Raven!" the fox said. He sounded friendly.

The raven, who was holding the cheese in his beak, did not answer.

"How handsome you look today!" the fox said. "Your coat of feathers is just as bright as a peacock's. And your eyes! They shine like two jewels!"

The raven began to stretch and preen himself.

"I like your beak best of all," the fox continued. "I can imagine how lovely your voice must be! I wish I could hear it!"

Dazzled by the fox's flattering words, the raven opened his beak and cawed as loud as he could.

The cheese dropped to the ground.

Laughing, the fox picked it up and ran away.

When the fox had
finished his story,
all the animals
except the raven
burst out laughing.

"That served the raven right!"
they cried.

But all the raven
could think about
was how to get even
with the fox.

The second tale
was told by the turtle.
It went like this:

There once was a hare who was always boasting of his great speed.

One day he met a turtle.

When he saw her short legs, he made fun of her.

But the turtle was not intimidated.

"Let's have a race," she said. "We'll see who runs faster."

"Gladly," the hare said, mockingly. "Do you really expect to win?"

"Yes," said the turtle.

They agreed on the course they would run and started together.

The hare ran off, laughing. He couldn't take this race seriously.

When he had run half the course, he lay down in the grass.

He had left the turtle so far behind that she was nowhere to be seen.

I might as well take a nap, he thought. I'll win anyway.

But the turtle kept walking straight ahead, one step at a time, without stopping.

By the time the hare started running again, the turtle had already come to the end of the course and was waiting for him.

When the turtle
had finished her story,
all the animals
except the raven and the hare
burst out laughing.

"That served the hare right!"
they cried.

But the hare went over
to stand next to the raven.
All he could think about
was how to get even
with the turtle.

The third tale
was told by the peacock.
It went like this:

There once was a crow who was very conceited. She despised all the other crows and was always trying to look more beautiful than she actually was.

One day she found some peacock feathers lying on the ground.

"That's just what I want," she said, and began to decorate herself with the feathers.

Thinking that no one would recognize her, she joined a group of peacocks.

But the beautiful birds were not deceived.

With loud cries, they attacked the crow and tore out her false feathers.

"Stop that! Leave me alone!" the crow screamed.

There she stood again as God had created her.

But when the peacocks discovered the crow's own glistening wing feathers, they said:

"You must have stolen those, too."

And they pecked and pecked at the crow until only a few scraggly feathers were left on her body.

When the peacock
had finished his story,
all the animals
except the raven,
the hare, and the crow
burst out laughing.

"That served the crow right,"
they cried.

But the crow went over
to stand next to
the hare and the raven.
All she could think about
was how to get even
with the peacock.

The fourth story
was told by the wolf.
It went like this:

There once was a wolf who was so hungry that his bones stood out from beneath his fur.

It was winter.

While hunting for food, he ran into a well-fed dog.

"I am stronger than you," said the wolf, "and yet I am nearly dying of hunger. How do you manage to get so fat?"

The dog felt flattered and replied:

"If you would serve my master, you could be just as well-off as I am. Plenty of meat and bones, and a full stomach with very little effort."

"How do you serve him?" asked the wolf.

"I watch the gate and protect his house from thieves," the dog replied. "Come with me!"

The snow is so deep, thought the wolf, and the air is so cold, even a wolf could use a roof over his head.

But as they trotted side by side, the wolf noticed a festering sore on the dog's neck.

"Who gave you that sore?" he asked.

"Oh, it's nothing," the dog said.

But the wolf kept asking.

Finally the dog answered sheepishly:

"I'm sore from the chain my master puts around my neck."

"In that case, go ahead and enjoy your food," said the wolf. "I'd rather stay hungry and be my own master."

When the wolf
had finished his story,
all the animals
except the raven, the hare,
the crow, and the dog
burst out laughing.

"That served the dog right!"
they cried.

But the dog went over
to stand next to
the crow, the hare,
and the raven.
All he could think of
was how he could get even
with the wolf.

Now the fox, the turtle,
the peacock, and the wolf
stopped laughing.
They stood facing the dog,
the crow, the hare,
and the raven,
whose only thoughts
were how to get even
with their enemies.

They started to fight,
first with words,
and then with their teeth
and beaks and claws.

The lovely meadow
became a battlefield.
One side appeared to be winning,
then the other.

But nearby, an old lion
lay sleeping in his den.
He woke up
and went to see
what all the noise was about.

When the fighting animals
saw the lion,
they fell silent.

The lion wanted to know
why they were fighting.
The raven, the hare,
the crow, and the dog
told him how the fox, the turtle,
the peacock, and the wolf
had made fun of them.

The lion listened attentively.
Then he, too, told a tale.
It went like this:

THE LION AND THE MOUSE

There once was a lion who was taking his midday nap.

Suddenly a mouse ran across his huge paws.

The lion woke up.

Annoyed at being disturbed, he seized the little creature and was about to devour it, when the mouse cried with a pitiful voice:

"King of the beasts, you are accustomed to fighting with bulls and stags. Look at me, I'm just a tiny tidbit for you. Let me live! Maybe I can repay you the favor someday."

The lion laughed and generously agreed to let the mouse go.

Not long after, he found himself caught in a hunter's net. He desperately tried to tear himself loose, but all his efforts were in vain.

The mouse, awakened by his roars, came out of her hole.

Without a moment's thought, she started to gnaw through the ropes with her sharp little teeth. And she didn't give up until the lion was free.

When the lion
had finished his story,
a little mouse who had seen
and heard everything
came out of her hole
and started whistling for joy.

Silently, the other animals
thought about the lion's story
and understood its meaning.

They decided to be friends again,
and the party continued
until early the next morning.
The fox danced with the raven,
the turtle with the hare,
the peacock with the crow,
the wolf with the dog,
and, of course, the lion
danced with the mouse.